game girl

Retro Whimsy
Book Three

sabrina cross

Copyright ©2025 by Sabrina Cross

 All Rights Reserved.

The characters and events portrayed in this book are fictitious. Any similarity to real persons, living or dead, is coincidental and not intended by the author.

No part of this book may be reproduced, or stored in a retrieval system, or transmitted in any form or by any means, electronic, mechanical, photocopying, recording, or otherwise without express written permission of the copyright owner. This title may not be entered into AI software or used for AI training purposes. For permission requests, email authorsabrinacross@gmail.com

Edited by: Writer's Wingman

Cover Design: Sabrina Cross

This book is 100% human made. No generative AI was used in the writing, editing, or production of this book.

 Formatted with Vellum

Ellie, Mia, & Michaela
Besties 5-Ever!

author's note

This is a sentient object romance. Humans will be getting it on with sentient objects. Don't worry, everyone is gleefully consenting.

If you read the last three sentences and think that's not for you, that's okay. There is still time to put this book down and walk away. No one will blame you. It's the sane thing to do.

But if you're going to stick around please be aware of the following: Cheating Ex, Magical Curses, Sexual Activity with Inanimate Objects, oral and vaginal sex, biting,

If you feel I am missing anything please reach out to me at authorsabrinacross@gmail.com and let me know. A complete list can be found at <u>www.sabrinacross.com</u>

one

. . .

"YOU HAVE to find your own hiding spot." I froze, hunched over in the doorway to the small plastic playhouse in my grandmother's backyard. "This one is mine."

"I brought tequila." I waved the bottle at my cousin. I caught her grin in the dim light before she held a hand out for the nearly full bottle of silver liquor.

"Now, this is why I've always liked you," Aubry said, lifting the bottle to her mouth. I dropped in the corner opposite her and crossed my legs. The space was tiny, and our knees rested against each other. "I know why I'm hiding, but why are you?"

I accepted the bottle back and took a swig of my own before answering. My wince was as much for the reasons I was hiding as it was for the burn of liquor. Honestly, at thirty I was too fucking old to be hiding in the kid's playhouse and drinking straight from the bottle. But, as Aubry's presence would indicate, sometimes it was necessary.

Don't get me wrong, I loved my family. They were great. They were also very traditional and loud. And there were just so freaking many of them. When you didn't meet the typical boilerplate outline of how one was supposed to live their life, they had opinions. So, so many opinions.

"I'll tell you mine if you tell me yours." I took another swig and handed the bottle back. Aubry accepted it with a nod and a 'go on' gesture. "I'm escaping the pity and recriminations. They're pretty torn between feeling sorry for me and blaming me for the fact Sean cheated on me and then publicly announced his engagement on his YouTube channel before he even bothered to break up with me."

"Fuck Katie, that's brutal." Aubry took a swig and winced before taking another one. "I'm hiding because I don't want to lie about still being single but I'm so not ready to tell them that I'm living with three men."

"I win." I took the bottle back from her.

"How do you figure? You think Grandma Jean is going to be accepting of a queer, polyamorous relationship?"

"Are you getting laid?" I took another drink and offered the bottle.

"Obviously." Her voice dripped with 'well, duh' as only an older cousin or sibling's voice could.

"Then I win. I haven't had sex in six weeks and I'm not sure that sex with Sean could have ever been called good."

"Why the hell were you with him then?" She handed back the bottle, and I thought about my answer while I drank.

"I guess I thought I loved him. I don't know. He was fun and we had a lot in common and it was comfortable." I shrugged and wished I had something better to explain wasting the last year of my life. The worst part was I didn't even miss him. I was angry because of the way he'd humiliated me and lied to me, but I wasn't upset by the loss of him. If he'd come to me and told me it was over, I wouldn't have fought him.

"You know the worst part? I can't even play video games anymore. He ruined them for me."

I loved gaming. The challenge of it, the community, the puzzles, and excitement. It had been something that brought us together in the beginning, but as he became more and more popular as a streamer he'd stopped wanting to play with me. He'd said I wasn't up to his level, and he didn't get anything from spending time together in-game. After my gamer tag leaked, most of the people who wanted to play with me online either wanted to tear me down for being with him or use me to get to him.

Aubry took the bottle back from me but didn't drink. She pointed the neck at me with a squinty-eyed look.

"You should play some older video games! Like the ones we played as kids. You used to kick all of our asses. It was fucking hilarious to see the boys lose their shit when you joined and destroyed them."

"I don't even have any of my old systems. I sold them." I shrugged. There wasn't any joy in gaming anymore. I didn't miss the old systems, and I highly doubted playing some retro video games was going to fix the fact I either had to give up online gaming entirely or start over fresh with a new gamer tag no one knew or could connect to my asshole ex.

"Have you been to Retro Whimsy? It's out in Old Town. I know they have some of the old systems and they didn't seem crazy expensive. I don't know. You know I suck at video games."

"Yeah, maybe." Neither of us said anything else

as we sat in the dark quiet, passing the bottle back and forth. We'd managed to finish off about half of it when a head poked through the open window and scared the crap out of me.

"They're looking for you," Aubry's brother Eric said with a grin. He was twenty-six to our thirty, and I was fairly certain he didn't have a serious bone in his body. "And Aunt Kay noticed the tequila was missing. She's got that look on her face like she's sucking lemons."

"If I start puking, can I go home?" I asked, only slightly joking.

"Not on your life, sister." Aubry said. She pushed to her knees and crawled out of the play-house. I handed the bottle to Eric through the window and crawled after her. We got to our feet, and I grabbed her arm for balance as the world started to tilt. She gripped my arm, and we stood there swaying together. I don't know who laughed first, but suddenly we were both laughing as we fought to stay upright.

"You guys are a mess." Eric said, sliding be-tween us and looping an arm around each of our waists. "Now, let's go inside so everyone can tell us what fuck ups we are."

"Okay," the world tilted as I trudged forward with the help of Eric's arm. "But I'm going to puke first, K?"

two

. . .

I DIDN'T VISIT Old Town very often. It was a quaint, touristy area filled with old buildings from the original town center before the city had expanded. It was an odd mix of historical significance mixed with kitschy shops and restaurants.

Aubry worked at an office building nearby and I'd thought about asking her to meet me for coffee and maybe come to the vintage store she recommended with me but then Sean had called about coming to get his stuff from the apartment and I'd spent the whole morning waiting for him because he hadn't been considerate enough to tell me what time he was coming over and refused to answer any of my texts asking for an ETA.

Honestly, until I'd pulled into the Old Town parking lot, I hadn't been convinced I was going. Sure, I'd love to get back into video games. They were my first love, and I hated that I'd let Sean take them away from me. I'd told myself all week it was a dumb idea and that I should just give in and create a new account, start over as someone new and not Sean's girlfriend who got publicly and humiliatingly dumped.

But Aubry's words had stuck with me. Maybe I should go back to the old school systems. Maybe it would be good for me to just play for the sake of playing and not worry about being social or stats or ranks. I'd spent so much time focusing on that stuff as Sean's girlfriend I'd lost the passion for playing.

The vintage store was easy enough to find. It was housed in a free-standing brick building with a green path access to one side and the parking lot on the other. Retro Whimsy was painted in the glass window in bold fonts and colors.

An old-fashioned bell rang over the door when I walked in, and the charm of it tickled me. It was a bright and airy space, with half the domed ceiling being made of glass. Cathedral windows ran along one side, overlooking the green path. There was a long glass display case acting as the checkout counter, though I didn't see anyone standing at there.

The store was broken into a number of little alcoves made from shelving and furniture. A row of free-standing clothing racks split the main aisle into two parts. A butter yellow leather sleeve caught my attention, and I made a mental note to stop at the racks after completing my mission to find the retro gaming systems.

"Hello!" A voice came from one of the alcoves. "Welcome to Retro Whimsy! Let me know if you need help finding anything!"

I could hear the exclamation point at the end of every sentence. The chipper sales clerk didn't instantly appear, so I picked a side of the clothing rack and started working my way toward the back.

Unlike Aubry, vintage stores weren't really my scene. I didn't enjoy poking through other people's cast-offs and the prize was never worth the effort, in my opinion.

"Hey, um, hi," I was unsure as I walked toward where the voice had come from. "I'm looking for some video game systems. My cousin said you might have some?"

A head popped out from an alcove a little over halfway down the long, somewhat narrow building. Her bright pink lips curled into a smile that turned into a grin when she saw me.

"Hey, we're almost twins!" She headed toward me as I tried to puzzle out what she meant. It only took a beat for me to see it. We both had hair nearly to our waist, though mine was a stick-straight copper while hers was a dark blond with goddess curls. My eyes were pale green compared to her bright blue. And while I was a perfectly average height at five-six, she had a few inches on me in height. Though I had a few sizes on her in curves.

I was wearing my traditional uniform of black leggings and a hoodie. My converse of the day were royal blue. She had on a flowy maxi dress in flowing rainbow colors and a tissue thin white, cropped, long-sleeve sweater.

"Well, maybe not twins but definitely of a type." She reached out and took my hand in both of hers. "Hi, I'm Addy, welcome!"

"Uh, yeah, thanks." I had no clue what to make of this overly familiar, excessively chipper woman. "It looks nice."

"Doesn't it?" She beamed at me, and I wanted to pull on sunglasses against the brightness of the look. "You said you were after video games?"

"Yeah, and the systems too." Addy started toward the back, keeping my hand grasped in hers.

She had a surprisingly firm grip as she hauled me through the store.

"We have them all! Is this for you or for a gift?" The back wall was lined with locked glass cabinets. Inside I could see all types of gaming systems from the old black and white handheld games to last Christmas' hottest system.

"Me," I said, idly looking over the games available. Maybe I would pick a game and decide on the system from there. "Trying to recapture my youth."

"You're too young to need to recapture your youth," she said it unironically, like she wasn't obviously the same age as me. "You should take the Square. It comes with a game already loaded in it."

I looked at the black box with a single remote control taped to the top. It had never been my favorite system, but maybe that's what I needed. None of the games on the shelves were jumping out at me. Maybe this was a dumb idea.

Before I made up my mind one way or the other, Addy was opening the display and pulling the system out. She double checked the remote and cords were all there and pressed it into my arms.

"Come on, I have the perfect jacket for you!" She gripped my arm and dragged me back toward the front of the store, toward the leather jacket that had caught my eye earlier.

three

. . .

"OKAY, this is going to be fun." I said, adjusting the TV to the correct input and turning on the Square. While it loaded, a task that took forever in the ancient system, I moved the armchair closer to the TV to accommodate the corded controller. The game that came with the system was clearly some bootlegged version. The tiny disc didn't have a label at all to indicate what was on it.

"And if it's not, I'll blame Aubry." I took a drink of my hard lemonade and set it on the coffee table before picking up the controller.

I needed to get a cat. At least then I could pretend I was talking to it, rather than talking to myself all the time. It was somewhat more socially acceptable to talk to cats, right? Sean hated cats and had always shut me down when I'd brought up the idea of getting one. Which was another reason I should have realized he was toxic and left him ages ago.

The black screen flickered to life with an unfamiliar logo. Three moons interlocked against a black background. There was no brand or company name under the logo. Weird.

The screen fades away, and a new one came up asking for my username. I thought about it for a moment before I chose a new gamertag. The one I'd worked so hard building for nearly a decade had been completely tainted by Sean, and I wanted a new start. The change felt bitter on my tongue as I typed it in. I shouldn't have been the one chased off the internet. I hadn't been the cheating liar. But hey, patriarchy was alive and well in gamer spaces.

After filling in my new username, I went through the steps to create a custom avatar of myself. The graphics were comically bad, and I couldn't help but laugh at how terrible they looked. Games sure had come a long way in the last decade.

Avatar complete, I was finally able to enter the game. There's no name, and it took me a moment to realize it was some sort of dating simulator.

My character was flocked by a group of handsome men in black masquerade masks. I rolled my eyes and debated changing to one of the other games I bought when I saw him in the background. He wasn't among the men flocking me, and he wasn't wearing a mask. He leaned against the wall with an arm propped behind his head.

He was tall and lean, with dark auburn hair and light green eyes. His face was all angles with an interesting bump on his nose that made me think it had been broken. His eyes caught mine, and he gave a small smile. It wasn't a happy expression, and that only made me more interested in him.

"Excuse me boys." I said aloud as I moved my avatar away from them and crossed the room to where the redheaded man waited. There were grumbles and sighs behind me from the rejected non-player characters.

What's a girl like you doing in a game like this? The redhead asked.

I frowned at the question. The character shouldn't know he's in a game. Shouldn't he have asked about the masquerade party we were at?

Three response options popped up on screen, and I picked the one that said NOWHERE ELSE I'D RATHER BE.

Desperation was probably closer to the honest answer, but that wasn't an option.

I can think of a few places I'd rather be.

The response was suggestive, but I almost imagined it wasn't. That the NPC was serious about wanting to be somewhere else. I shook off the thought as fanciful and focused back on the screen.

The man held out his hand, and options flashed on screen.

REJECT HIM, ACCEPT A DANCE, TAKE A MOONLIGHT STROLL.

They all sounded so cheesy, and I kind of delighted in selecting the dance option.

Sean would never dance with me. He told me it was because I had two left feet, but I knew it was because he hated dancing and just wouldn't admit it. I swallowed back the rising anger at him and at myself for taking his abuse for so long.

The scene changed, and we were in the middle of a large ballroom with swirling couples. Ballgown skirts billowed out and surrounded the legs of the dancing couples. I tried to look down to see what I was wearing, but the view didn't allow it.

May I have this dance? The man asked.

I took his outstretched hand. The view zoomed out, and I could see my avatar in a light green dress swirling along with the redheaded man.

I continued to play the game until the romance

line ended with the man proposing to me. I smiled as he rose from one knee to press a kiss to my forehead.

"At least someone likes me enough to propose." I said to myself as I turned off the console and sat the remote down. I glanced at my watch and was shocked to learn three hours had gone by as I played.

It was almost eleven at night, and I had to work in the morning. I took care of my hard lemonade bottle and got ready for bed.

four

. . .

A HANGOVER KICKED my ass the next morning. I'd only had the one drink, so I should have been fine, but I dragged all through work. And working from home meant it took all my effort not to just crawl back into bed between meetings and catch up on sleep.

I was a dedicated early to bed, early to rise sort of person. And I couldn't believe I had stayed up as late as I had, playing a silly dating sim that felt like it was set in Regency England.

Work dragged on endlessly and I felt like it would never end. By the time I closed out the last call of the day and shut down my station, I was starving and ready for bed. But after making myself a frozen dinner of chicken and rice, I found myself feeling restless.

Nothing caught my attention and I almost called Aubry before I remembered she was dating three men and was probably too busy for me right now. Especially because no one in our family had taken the announcement well, and she was probably still dealing with the fallout with her mother. My aunt threatened to call the priest in to counsel her. More like to perform an exorcism, I thought.

I could call my brother, but he was more of a mess than me most days. And I didn't have it in me to be his therapist. I once again got angry at Sean. Not only had he stolen my future, but he'd alienated me from my friends, both online and in person.

Thinking of him had my anger spiking, and I found myself going back to the Square console and turning on the game again. I would just play for a little bit until I was ready for sleep.

This time when I logged in, I wasn't at a masquerade ball but some sort of rave with neon lights and thumping bass. I could almost feel the music pulse through me, even though I had the sound down low enough I could barely hear it.

"Okay, weird." I mumbled to myself as the game started.

I'm approached by a dark-haired man in a bright yellow fishnet shirt and tight leather shorts who asked me to dance. I turn him down and work my way through the room looking for the red-headed character from the night before. I don't know why I was convinced I would find him, but when I spotted him, my heart skipped a beat.

He's wearing a pair of tight leather pants and knee-high leather boots with a super tight white shirt that glowed under all of the black and neon lights. He had a pair of glow glasses on his head and looked utterly drool worthy standing against a pillar in the back of the room.

Fancy seeing you here.

He said in chat. I grinned and moved to stand beside him.

What brings you out tonight? He asked.

Lonely. I typed into the chat box. It was a slow process to use the joystick to select each letter individually. Honestly, I was a little shocked the game had a chat for a single-player, closed-universe game. It shouldn't have.

I forgot my question about the chat option when he held out his hand again.

DANCE, OR GO SOMEWHERE QUIET.

I selected to go somewhere quiet and watched as he led my avatar, wearing a tight denim skirt and a jaggedly ripped white tank top covered in neon splotches, out of the room and up onto the second floor of the warehouse.

I can help you escape your loneliness, but only for a little while.

It sounded like a come-on line. But then he laid down and pulled me with him to look at the fairy lights strung along the rafters.

I'm not sure what I expected next, but it wasn't the repeated games of Never Have I Ever or 20 Questions that went on until the wee hours of the morning.

You should sleep. He told me.

I glanced at my watch, it was almost midnight. I'd lost hours in the game again.

I'll be here when you need me.

The words flashed across the screen just before it went black. I put the remote away and vowed to stop playing. There's getting lost in games and then there's whatever had just happened to me. I couldn't keep staying up all night playing video games.

five

. . .

I DIDN'T PLAY the Square for the rest of the week, but then Saturday rolled around and I found myself bored with nothing to do. I figured it couldn't hurt. I would set an alarm and keep it to a reasonable hour of play time.

This time when the game loaded, I found myself at what looked like a vampire ball. Everyone was dressed in dramatic red and black and Victorian style was everywhere. Someone handed me a fluted glass of some sort of red liquid.

I wouldn't drink that unless you're prepared to embrace the eternal night.

I turned to see the red-haired man standing beside me. He wore fitted black pants with tall boots and a loose-fitted poet's top unlaced to show off his bare chest.

Hello again.

I hand the glass off to a passing tray and accept the offer of a dance from the man.

Do you have a name? I ask in the chat box as we swirled around the dance floor.

Nathaniel.

I repeated the name aloud and let it roll around in my mouth. It was a good name.

I played the game through until Nathaniel turned me into his vampire bride. When I came back to myself, my eyes were dry and itchy in a way they shouldn't have been. I check my phone. It's one in the morning, and my alarm had been shut off. I had no memory of doing it.

"What the fuck?" I asked the room as I cleaned up my space and got myself a much-needed glass of water. That game was dangerous.

I couldn't explain it, but it wasn't like I was playing a game. It felt like I was in the game and really there with Nathaniel. I laughed at myself for such an absurd thought and got ready for bed.

But when I woke up the next morning, I couldn't help but feel the pull of the game and the man inside of it. I wanted to know what scenario we would be put into next. I couldn't resist the draw of the game. I got water and snacks and turned on the Square.

Back again so soon? You can't keep hiding from re-ality in video games. It leads to nothing but trouble. Nathaniel told me as he came to my side at the country-western bar. He wrapped his arm around my waist without a prompt. Which part of me reg-istered, but the rest of me was excited to see where the adventure would lead.

This one was hotter than any of the other story-lines. Nathaniel kept his hands on my body as he twirled me around the dance floor. They strayed south until I could almost feel the pressure of them on my lower back with the tops of his fingers brushing my ass. His lips pressed into my neck on the quiet deck under the moonlight, and I swore I could feel the sensation on my own body.

It was ridiculous, and I knew it. It had just been a long while since the last time Sean and I had sex. And I hadn't been taking care of myself as often as usual. It was the only reason that playing a video game was getting me turned on. But when the remote started to vibrate in my hand with choices, I couldn't stop myself from pressing the curved end against my clit.

That's it, darlin'. Ride me. Nathaniel said on screen.

It wasn't in context with the action in the game.

"What the fuck?" I said out loud. I removed the handheld from between my legs and tossed it on the floor.

You're stopping? It was just starting to get good, KatieKat.

"Oh, this is not happening." I ran my hands through my hair and tangled them in the strands at the back of my head. It was absolutely insane. The video game was not interacting with me. Sure, it wasn't like any other game I'd ever played before, but it wasn't interacting with me. It couldn't. Video games did not interact with players like that. They also did not attempt to fuck players.

I wish I could agree with you, but I've been stuck here for years and have had plenty of time to accept the reality of it.

"What do you mean you've been there for years?"

My girlfriend decided that if I like video games so much, I should be one. That was in two-thousand-fourteen. I'm not sure how long I've been here, but you're the first person to pick me up.

Eleven years. He'd been a game for eleven years. My god. I shook myself. No, that couldn't be true. There was no way to curse someone into a game. That was Hollywood shit. Hell, even Hollywood had never done anything so ridiculous that I could think of.

"That's ridiculous."

You're talking to a video game.

He had a point there. Okay, okay. Maybe I could believe this.

six

. . .

WHAT ARE *the odds of me getting you to finish what you started?*

"Absolutely none." Any sexy feelings I'd had were long gone with the sheer shock of what Nathaniel, the video game character, was saying. It was absolutely insane. But I couldn't argue that he was talking to me and seemed to be able to hear the words I was saying.

Damn shame. Not as good as sex, but it felt nice. I get it though. It's late, KatieKat. You should get some sleep.

I glance at my phone and note it's nearly ten. Earlier than I'd been going to sleep but late enough that I'd be feeling it in the morning.

"You're right. I need to sleep. And think." I went to turn the game off and stopped. "What happens to you when I turn this off?"

Nothing.

"Oh, good." I reach for the power button, but a new message flashes on the screen.

I mean nothing. I revert to nothing. The game goes black, and I'm stuck in the dark until the next time the game turns back on. Would you be willing to leave it on until the next time? He looks around the country bar and shrugs. *This isn't really my scene, but it's better than darkness.*

My heart breaks a little at the thought of him being stuck in blackness for over a decade. I would have been absolutely insane.

"Yeah, I can do that." I tell him before turning the volume off. The light wouldn't bother me from my bedroom, but the sound would. I clean up my drinks and snacks and head to bed.

I dreamed of Nathaniel at the Vampire Ball. The candlelight that flickered across his auburn hair and put shadows in his eyes. He spun me around the dance floor, my dress twirling around us.

"Help me, Katie," he whispered against my neck. "Save me."

His lips closed over my pulse point, and I tilted my head to give him better access. Nathaniel's lips ran up and down the column of my neck before he returned to my pulse point. I gripped his upper arms and rode the pleasure of his kisses.

Just when I was about to beg him to kiss me, he struck. His fangs dug deep into my neck, and blood began welling up.

I screamed, and everything went black. I sat up in bed and shuddered as my heart beat against my ribcage. My breathing was ragged and harsh. When my hand moved up to my neck, the flesh was tender. But no blood came away.

A dream, a bad dream. It was just a dream. I repeated the words to myself as I pulled my socks on and got out of bed.

In the kitchen, I poured myself a glass of water and downed it in four large gulps. It helped settle my breathing and racing heart. I refilled the glass and took it with me into the living room.

The TV was still on. Light flickered oddly as the country bar continued to dance and drink. My gaze flicked around the screen until I spotted Nathaniel in the bottom corner. He sat by himself at a booth with a glass bottle of beer in front of him. He was picking at the label with a serious expression on his digital face.

Was he really a human cursed into a game? Had he been able to keep a shred of sanity being stuck in the dark for the last decade? I couldn't see how.

The dream left me feeling unsettled and uncertain. I was about to go back to bed when words flashed across the screen.

Can't sleep?

"Not so much." I didn't mention my weird dream. But I approached the TV with caution.

Can I help?

"You've been keeping me from sleeping more than anything lately."

Is that why you stayed away for so long?

I sat in the chair in front of the TV and picked up the controller. I toyed with the joystick idly without really moving it.

"Some of it." I didn't want to admit I was becoming addicted to him. To his game. To him? It's all a jumble inside of me and kept me from admitting anything.

I'm glad you came back. He looked up from the label, and his eyes met mine. It was impossible, and yet, I couldn't deny what was happening.

"I should get back to bed." I told him. The controller vibrated in my hands. I took that as a rejection of the idea. But Nathaniel's face remained placid.

Sweet dreams, KatieKat.

"You can just call me Katie." KatieKat22 was the

handle I'd picked to start my new gaming experience. It wasn't very clever or attention grabbing, like my last gamer tag but it would do.

I like KatieKat. I waited for him to go on, but he just went back to picking at the label on the bottle. *Goodnight.*

"Goodnight." I left the living room and went back to bed. Nothing about the interaction was weird, other than the talking to a video game character, but something felt different.

I lay awake long into the night trying to figure out what was bothering me.

seven

. . .

GOOD MORNING, *KatieKat.*

The message greeted me on my screen when I left the bedroom the next morning. I'd almost convinced myself the whole thing was a crazy fever dream, but the proof of it was there across my screen.

"Morning," I croaked out on my way to the kitchen and the much needed caffeine that lived there. I grabbed an energy drink from the fridge and, because there was no time to make breakfast, I grabbed a protein shake as well. I cracked the top of the energy drink and took both with me as I shuffled toward the second bedroom, that acted as my office.

How are you this morning?

"Tired. Gotta work. Back later."

I stumbled my way into the office and booted up my computer. Work wouldn't wait, no matter how much I needed the time for the caffeine to kick in.

All day long my mind kept wandering back to the television and the man inside the game. Could I believe him? A decade inside a video game for being a crappy boyfriend seemed a little excessive. But then again, people were crazy. So I couldn't dismiss it.

Which led me to my second question. Was there a way to get him out of the video game? Could he be saved? What kind of life would he have to come back to if he's been gone so long? A person could be declared legally dead after seven years. He could even legally not exist anymore.

Still, if I could help him, wasn't I morally required to? I supposed I could return him to Retro Whimsy and tell the salesperson, but she would probably just think I was crazy.

No, it was up to me to help him. I just had to figure out how.

———

By the time I finished work that afternoon, I was no closer to having any idea of how to free Nathaniel. I was also barely more awake than when I started the day. I trudged out of my office with the empty cans and crossed to the kitchen.

Words flashed across the silent TV screen, but I didn't stop to read them. Caffeine and food first. I pulled another energy drink from the fridge and popped the top as I looked through the cupboards. Nothing caught my eye, so I grabbed a cup of noodles.

Once that was in the microwave, I wandered back toward the living room and the game. No message awaited me on the screen, but I spotted Nathaniel instantly. He laid on top of the bar, stretched out with his feet crossed at the ankles and his hat over his face.

"I thought you didn't sleep." I said, leaning

against the side of the couch. Nathaniel lifted his hat and turned his head to look at me.

I don't. The words stretched across the screen. *But I am beginning to go a little crazy in this bar. Country isn't my thing, and they've been playing the same five songs all day.*

Okay, I would probably be trying to zone out at that point too. The microwave beeped, and I stepped back and into the kitchen for my food. I grabbed a plastic fork off the counter and the noodles out of the microwave before I headed back into the living room with my energy drink.

I settled into the chair in front of the TV and set my drink on the end table.

Can you do me a favor? I took a bite of noodles and nodded, assuming he could see me. I'm proven right when new words scroll out. *Turn the system off and restart the game? I'll take just about anything different at this point.*

"Your wish is my command." I leaned forward and pressed the button before I could think better of it. I held my breath as I waited for the screen to light back up. The breath released in a whoosh when the loading screen started. I selected my game and waited for it to load. This time I found myself standing outside a large, dilapidated Victorian mansion. No one was there, so I brought my character inside the main room.

WELCOME TO THE HAUNTED MANSION! FIND YOUR WAY THROUGH, BUT BEWARE, THE BEINGS THAT HAUNT THESE HALLS WON'T BE AS PLEASED TO SEE YOU.

Oh, cool. Except I had no clue where to find Nathaniel. Would he be one of the scare actors? That could be hot, actually.

I set the controller down and finished my cup of

noodles and energy drink. After taking care of my trash and grabbing a water, I sat back down and returned to the game.

I was maybe ten minutes into exploring the house when my controller started vibrating and someone jumped out at me. I jumped, and then cursed when the character removed an old-school hockey mask to reveal his face.

"Fuck, Nathaniel, you scared the crap out of me."

Kind of the point, kitten.

I scowled at the TV.

He just laughed. *Not what I expected, but better than the country bar. How are you tonight?*

"Tired. Going to have to call it early." I toyed with the joystick, unsure what to say.

Can you stay for a while?

"A little while."

We wandered around the haunted house, and I jumped at nearly every scare. I hadn't realized I was such a scaredy cat. I didn't even jump that hard at real haunted houses. I guessed I was just on edge.

"Do you know how to get out of there?" I blurt out. We're standing in a closet where no one can jump out at us. I stretched my back out against the chair and tried to relax my muscles, but I was wound so tight.

Not a clue. But thanks for wanting to.

He traced a finger down my cheek and neck, and I can practically feel it on my skin. I brought my hand up to trace the path he had taken, feeling the ghost of his touch on me.

"It doesn't seem fair." I said, wishing I could touch him as well, but it wasn't a prompt in the game. So I just stared at the angles of his face and imagined.

I learned a long time ago, life isn't fair. Nathaniel's hand came up to cup my avatar's face. *For example, here you are. I can see you. I can hear you. I can even almost touch you. And yet, you're entirely out of my reach.*

He leaned forward and pressed his lips to my avatar's and I swore I could feel the brush of his lips on mine.

I wonder how you'd taste. This is just electricity, energy. It's not real, and yet it feels like the most real thing to happen to me in years.

His fingers wrapped in the avatar's hair, and I felt the tug in mine. I gasped, and his face swung away from my digital form to the screen. To me.

"Do that again." I ordered, gripping the controller tightly in both hands and waiting for the tug against my scalp. His fist tightened, and I could feel it. The ghost of a tug. Almost there, but not quite.

Can you feel that? Can you feel me, KatieKat?

eight

· · ·

IMPOSSIBLY, I could. I could feel the tug of his fist in my hair. When he crashed his mouth down onto my digital form, I could feel that too. A pressure, a spark. It wasn't a kiss, not really. But it felt like something.

His hands skimmed down the digital body and back up again to cup my breasts. I gasped again, sensation pressing against me but not quite. Not enough.

Nathaniel's eyes were open and on me, through the screen. I didn't bother to hide my reaction to him. I lifted one hand to close over my breast, over the ghost touch of his.

I can't feel you. I need to feel you. His face was the picture of frustration, and he pushed away from the digital me to focus entirely on me through the screen.

"How?" I asked, wanting to feel him more.

The remote. Try the remote. I looked down at the hunk of plastic in my hand, unsure what he meant. The remote began to vibrate gently, the way it did when something was about to happen on screen.

This time, though, it was vibrating for something about to happen in reality. If I let it.

After a moment's hesitation, I dropped the remote to my lap. Disappointment flashed over Nathaniel's face, gone almost as quick as it appeared.

I understand. The words flashed across the screen.

But no, he didn't understand. Not yet.

With a deep breath, I tugged my shirt over my head and dropped it onto the carpet next to me. Because I'd woken up late, I'd never bothered to put on a bra, and my breasts hung heavy against my torso.

Nathaniel's eyes went wide, and then dark. His gaze travelled over me, and one hand reached up to brush against the avatar's chest. It felt like a feather across my nipple, and I couldn't stop the shudder.

More. The word a demand. A plea. I could read the desperation on Nathaniel's face as he kept his eyes locked on me through the screen.

I lifted the vibrating controller and ran it down my sternum, between my breasts and back up again. It looked like Nathaniel groaned as I moved the controller outward toward one peaked tip. This time a shudder went through him at the same time it pulsed through me. The ghost touch tightened on my other breast, and I let out a moan.

The way you sound…

He didn't have to finish the sentence for me to understand that he liked the sounds I made. So when I pressed the remote harder to one breast while I pinched my other nipple, I didn't hold back the moan like I might have. Sean had always been so worried about being overheard or insisted it was distracting. It felt so good to just let it out without worry.

"Can you feel me?" I asked him as I circled the point of the handle against my chest. The vibration sped up and got harder.

Almost. It's not enough. I need more.

This time I didn't hesitate. I dropped the controller to the floor and rose. It took a single pull of the tie at my waist and then a quick shove, my pants and underwear were around my ankles. I was still kicking them off as I reached for the controller again.

The vibration almost hurt my hand as I slid it across my belly and down. I wanted to tease myself and Nathaniel, so instead of immediately putting it where I wanted it, I slid the controller to my knee, down the top of my leg.

Show me. The words flashed red on the screen, and the vibration impossibly sped up.

I relented and gave us what we both wanted. I spread my legs wide and tossed one over the arm of the chair. I slowly slid the remote up the inside of my thigh to the patch of curls at the apex.

Fucking beautiful. His eyes were rapt on me. He no longer touched the avatar me, but instead his hands were on his belt buckle. He slowly pulled it undone as he watched me.

My eyes were glued on their motions as I slid the remote higher. But when the hard plastic, warmed from my hands, made contact with my pussy, I couldn't maintain the contact. My eyes fluttered shut as a loud gasp escaped me.

I turned it and tilted the U-shaped handle until the tight-curved edge of it was placed against my clit. The vibrations sung through me until I was crying out.

The steady vibrations started coming in bursts, and I dragged my lids open and to the screen. The words *Oh Fuck* flashed over and over again as Nathaniel moved his hand over his cock.

The game graphics weren't fantastic, and I couldn't quite make out what he was working with, but it looked like it might be impressive. I wanted to close my eyes and give into imagination, but the way he looked at me kept me from looking away.

"I wish you were inside of me," I told Nathenial. My breaths came in pants as I worked the controller over me. I pressed down on my clit and moaned loudly.

The controller heated up in my hand until I had to drop it. The screen flashed red as Nathaniel's hand moved rapidly over his cock.

Now! The word flashed over and over again. I reached for the controller, but it was so hot to touch. There was almost a shimmering haze around it. I reached for it again and quickly drew my hand back as it began to vibrate in place on the floor.

I watched with growing fascination as the controller began to shift. The thumb joystick, usually the size of a dime, pushed out from the handle and grew until the head was just smaller than a fifty cent piece. It flared out around a base just slightly smaller.

"Did…did my controller just grow a cock?"

Did I care?

The shimmer disappeared, and it stopped vibrating. I couldn't stem my curiosity. I grabbed the controller and rubbed my thumb over the velvety smooth pad of the joystick. It began to vibrate again, and I knew what I was going to do.

"This is the worst idea in the history of bad

ideas," I told Nathaniel as I shifted to my knees on the floor in front of the chair.

Best. Best idea. Take it. Take me.

The screen was still flashing a bright red, so bright it almost hurt my eyes to watch, but I didn't look away as I dropped to one hand and moved the controller between my legs. I positioned the new, larger joystick at my entrance.

The controller vibrated in my hand as I slowly shifted and sank down onto it. It spread me wide, too fast. Much faster than an actual cock would. The joystick was now about half the width of my fist at the top. The pressure at my entrance was intense, but I persisted until it pressed inside of me.

I threw my head back with a moan as I slid it further inside. "Fuck. Oh fuck," It was a chant as I worked it deeper until my pussy lips met the base of the controller. The vibrations sung through me, and I ground down.

One of the buttons popped up and pressed against my clit. I screamed. I couldn't help it. I was so full. The vibrations were hitting just right. The orgasm washed over me shockingly fast, and I could do nothing but ride it out.

nine

. . .

THE CONTROLLER HEATED up inside of me. The pain of it was almost unbearable, and I scrambled up to my knees to reach between my legs to grab the controller.

But an aftershock hit me and shook my entire body until I fell forward. Sobs wracked my body as I curled my fingers into the carpet and fought through the pain and pleasure that warred inside of me.

My eyes were clenched tight but flew open when the controller began to shift again.

"Oh fuck," I needed it out of me. I reached down to pull it out, but the wave of heat nearly burned my fingers. I was going to have burns in my vagina. There was no way I could explain this to the EMTs.

The vibrations kicked up again, and my vagina clenched around it. But it felt different. It wasn't the hard plastic of the joystick but the firm push of a cock. I dragged my eyes open to look down to see a body forming. The controller was fading away to hips. The heat shimmered beneath me as legs and a torso formed.

My eyes flew to the screen, but Nathaniel wasn't there anymore. The entire screen was black.

I looked back down at the body forming beneath me, inside of me. Fuck it was so fucking weird. And hot.

Not the good kind of hot. Not the kind of hot that seared the skin and burned. The kind of hot that left an ache. And it just kept getting hotter, and the pain kept getting more intense.

I tried to push up with my legs, but I couldn't move. I was frozen in place, forced to endure the agony of whatever was happening beneath me.

My body arched, and my head flew back. I let out a scream as the heat overwhelmed me. I pushed against the floor, expecting the rough carpet but my hands met burning flesh instead.

Tilting my head down toward the wave of fire, I found myself looking into pale green eyes instead of industrial grey carpet.

"What the fuck?" I yelled, pushing away. Hands gripped my hips but then immediately released me as the heat abated. I was finally able to scrabble off the controller that was no longer a controller–now a tall, attractive, very naked man.

"Good question." The man, Nathaniel, it had to be Nathaniel, said.

No longer a pixilated image using decade old graphics but flesh and blood. He sat up, pulling one leg to his chest and wrapped his arms around it.

"What? How?" My mind was spinning, but I couldn't deny that he was here. I reached out and touched his calf, warm and firm under my finger. "Huh?"

"I don't know." Nathaniel looked back to the screen, which now was holding steady on the main menu. "I never expected– I didn't know– Wow."

He looked back to me, his eyes wide and bright as he looked over my naked body. Something I had actually managed to forget about in all of the insanity. "Thank you."

I had no clue what he was thanking me for. I hadn't done anything. I didn't understand what was happening. All I knew was my skin was still on fire and the man in front of me had just been inside of me and I could still feel the imprint of him there.

Shaking my head, I reached for the console and turned it off, half expecting Nathaniel to disappear. Instead, the screen blinked to black and I watched as he let out a sigh of relief.

"Okay, so you're really here." I poked his leg again, and he reached out to grab my hand. "Is this a permanent thing?"

"I have no idea." He tugged gently on my hand, an encouragement to come closer but not a forceful movement that left me feeling vulnerable. Which was crazy, given that I was naked with a complete stranger who had just transformed from a game controller after I'd fucked it.

"How do you feel?" I asked. His skin was warm but no longer scalding hot.

His hand flexed in mine, and he ran his other hand down his torso and up to rest on his chest, over his heart. A grin formed on his face as he sat there.

"Amazing. I have a pulse again!" He tugged me forward, pressing my hand to his chest beneath his. "Holy shit, I'm alive again!"

ten

. . .

I WASN'T PREPARED for the kiss when he swooped down and pressed his lips to mine in a large, smacking smooch. It seemed to surprise him as much as it did me. "I'm sorry."

He started to pull away. But, as crazy as it was, I didn't want him to. I reached my free hand up to his shoulder and pulled him toward me until I could kiss him.

It only took him a second to respond. A second before he released my hand on his chest and drove his hand into my hair. He fisted the strands and tilted my head back to an angle he liked. I licked out, tracing the line of his lips, and he opened to me on a groan.

"Fuck Katie," he released my hair, and his hands moved to my waist. A moment later I was airborne as he lifted me over his hips to settle on his thighs. His cock was pressed against my mound and poked into the curve of my belly. It throbbed against me, and I couldn't help but remember what it felt like inside of me.

"Can I touch you?" The question threw me at first. We were naked, I was straddling his lap, my tongue was down his throat. Of course he could touch me.

Except his hands were still wrapped around my waist, just below my boobs. His thumbs were braced just below the curve, and the slightest movement would have him caressing me.

"Yes." I placed my hand over his and slid it up, over the curve of my tit until his palm pressed against my nipple. "Touch me."

His fingers flexed, and he squeezed before letting out a low groan. He eyed my flesh as I released him and let him trace a fingertip around my hard nipple.

"It's been ten years since I've really felt anything. Touch in the game is like running your hand next to an electric fence. Sometimes you get a bit of a shock, but mostly it's just the impression of touch." His eyes flicked up to mine, held. "Touching you feels kind of the same. Hot, so hot. But soft. And when we spark, it's not going to hurt. It's going to burn."

He brought his lips back to mine in a searing kiss at the same time his fingers closed around my nipple. I gasped at the rough touch, and he invaded my mouth with his tongue.

His other hand slid down to grip my hip, and he used it to pull me forward until I was nestled tight against his cock. He rocked me back, and I instantly understood.

I brought my hands to his shoulders for balance and held on as I began to rock over his cock. The length of it slid along my slick folds, hot and hard. I whined into his mouth as the head caught against my hot button over and over again with my movements.

His hand fell away from my boob and dropped

to my hip so he could use both hands to guide me in a quick, hard rhythm against him.

"I want to fuck you." I moaned against his mouth. "I need you inside me again."

"Can't." The word was guttural against my mouth. "If I get inside you, this is all over. And I need it to last."

I whined, but he didn't relent. He just kept moving me over his lap until the slickness of my cunt mixed with the beading precum of his cock. The soundtrack of the moment was slick skin, low groans, and desperate moans as I rode over him.

"Please, please please," I begged, rocking back and forth over his cock. "I need you inside of me."

In a flash, Nathaniel rolled us until I was beneath him. My breath hitched at the casual show of strength. It stopped when he pressed against my opening with the tip of his cock.

He groaned before he pushed up and away from me. I clawed at his shoulders, trying to bring him back where I wanted him.

"Nathaniel," I whined.

"Shhh KatieKat, I'll give you what you need." He pressed a kiss to my forehead before slowly dragging himself down my body. His lips pressed against my jaw, between my breasts, against my belly and down, down, down until the heat of his breath fanned against my already wet folds.

I arched up into him. He grabbed me behind my knee and drew one leg up over his shoulder. His other hand rested on my thigh to spread me wide. So wide.

"Fuck, prettiest pussy I've ever seen." Nathaniel blew a breath over the wet skin and sent a shiver through my body. Before I could comment, he dipped his head and licked a path from my opening to my clit.

I moaned and arched back as he circled the sensitive bud with the tip of his tongue. He latched on with his lips and sucked my clit into his mouth.

It struck me that I should be the one bringing him pleasure. Sure, my sex life with my ex wasn't great, but I'd at least had sex in the last six months, let alone the last ten years. As good as it felt to have his mouth on me, I wanted to make him feel good even more.

"I want your cock in my mouth," I said. He groaned into my pussy, which sent shockwaves through my body. I gripped his hair and tugged.

"Let me taste you." I told him, trying to be firm. It didn't come across well when he slid one finger inside of me and made my body bow.

"Sorry, I'm a little busy right now." He pulled against my grip in his hair.

"You don't have to. I want to make you feel good."

"Katiekat, there is nothing I want more right now than to feast on you." His eyes were clouded with pleasure, and I realized he wasn't doing this just for my sake as some twisted thank you for freeing him. He actually liked eating me. "Now, let me get back to the first meal I've had in a decade."

I released my grip and dug my nails into his shoulders instead as he dipped his head to lick at my clit, the same time he moved that one finger in and out of me, twisting it to add friction.

"I could suck you while you fuck me." I offered. Now that the idea was in my head, I'd realized I wanted it. I wanted his cock in my mouth. I wanted to know what he tasted like.

"Look Kitten, I know it's been a while but there

is no way I'm going to be able to give this pussy the attention it deserves if your mouth is wrapped around my cock. Why don't we take turns? I'll make you feel so fucking good, then you can have what you want."

"Seems like I'm getting the better end of this bargain." I shifted up to my elbows to look down my body at him. He looked up at me with serious green eyes.

"You'd be wrong. Very wrong." With that, he dropped his head again, and it was on. There was no letting me stop him. He was a man determined. And his focus was all about making me feel good.

One finger inside me became two. And before long, he was stretching me with three long fingers inside of me. My legs were restless on the carpet as I fought for control.

Nathaniel was relentless in his assault on my clit. And when he found the pressure I needed and paired it with a firm rub on my g-spot, I was a goner.

I came hard, liquid spurting out of me and covering his entire hand and face. It was unlike anything I'd ever experienced before in my life.

The pleasure was so intense, so acute, it actually bordered on painful. He kept it up, slowly stroking and licking as I came down from the biggest high of my life.

"Jesus fuck," Nathaniel said, bringing his soaked hand to his face to lick at his fingers. "That was…"

"Embarrassing." I filled in. I covered my face with my hands to hide from the complete mess I'd made of him with my orgasm.

"The most beautiful thing I've ever experienced." Nathaniel tugged my hands away from my face and pressed a kiss to my lips. I could taste me on him. "Thank you."

I laughed. I couldn't help it. "You're thanking me for the best, most intense orgasm I've ever had?"

"I could say the same." I glanced down and noticed his cock was going soft between his legs. I cocked an eyebrow at him, and he tilted his head until I noticed the damp spot on the carpet. Well, the second one, about three feet lower than the one I'd left.

"Did you just…"

"Come from eating you out? Abso-fucking-lutely."

I wouldn't consider myself particularly adventurous in bed, but I'd had my fair share over the years. And not once has anything made me as hot as knowing that Nathaniel came to my cum.

"That's…" I was without words. Instead, I wrapped my hand around the back of his neck and pulled him down until I could kiss him again.

He tangled his hands in my hair and kissed me like it was the last time. The thought sobered me. Maybe it was the last time he would kiss me. We'd barely spoken, let alone confirmed he'd want to ever see me again.

I pulled away and released him. Something flashed across his face, a little dark, before it was gone again.

"I think we could use a shower." I said, pushing to my feet. Wanting to make the night last as long as I could, I held out my hand to him, "Care to join me?"

eleven

. . .

MY SHOWER WAS PRETTY standard sized, with more than enough room for one average-sized woman but not so much for an average-sized woman and a nearly six-foot-tall former video game character.

"Sorry," I said, smooshing myself against the wall so he could get under the spray and rinse the soap off. He had to bend over to get the shampoo out of his hair, and I took the opportunity to enjoy the view of his ass. He had a really nice one.

As soon as the water ran free from soap, he stood up and wrapped an arm around my waist. He pulled me against him, under the warm spray of water.

"Closed spaces have some benefits." He ran his hands down my back and over the curve of my ass. He pulled me up until I was on my toes and pressed against his hard, lean body.

I was about to object when his mouth closed over mine. I lost myself to the kiss and the caress of his hands over my body. He snaked one down, down until he could press his fingers inside of me. My pussy was still sensitive from earlier

"You may have a point," I panted as he probed inside of me with seeking fingers. I gripped his shoulders as my legs began to shake.

"I'm a fucking genius," He said against my neck as he drove me up to the edge with his wicked fingers. "Are you going to come for me, kitten?"

"Thinking about it." My nails dug into his shoulders as I ground myself down against his hand.

He twisted his wrist and pressed down against my g-spot at the same time his thumb came up to press against my clit. It was all over for me. I came with a cry that echoed around the tiled space.

Nathaniel slid his fingers free as I came down. I clung to his shoulders as he turned us so I was under the brunt of the cooling spray.

When I tried to slide my hand down his chest to reciprocate, he stopped me. "It's alright kitten."

After he pressed a kiss to my palm, he got out of the shower and left me there feeling all kinds of confused. I finished washing up, and when I got out, Nathaniel had left the bathroom.

Maybe he didn't want me. He wouldn't be the first guy to take a good look at me and decide I wasn't enough. Nathaniel was hot, just released from a curse, and would have all kinds of options. Heck, maybe he wanted to track down his old girlfriend and see if they could make up.

I took my time in the bathroom as I dried off and got ready for bed. I did the full body routine I usually only managed on weekends. I hoped that by the time I got out of the bathroom, either Nathaniel would have left or would have had time to decide what he wanted to do next.

Whatever it is, I'd support him in it. It was the least I could do.

My bedroom was empty when I walked in. I quickly dressed in a pair of joggers and a tank top before heading down the hall. I found Nathaniel in my second bedroom-slash-office. He was sitting at my desk with a game controller in his hands.

"What's this?" He asked me, holding up the controller. He used it to wave at my set up and I felt my stomach drop. Of course he'd be interested in my streaming setup. What gamer guy wouldn't be?

My rig wasn't the top of the line, but it was pretty fucking nice. I'd been a rising streamer when I'd met Sean, and I'd played alongside him for a while before he felt he was beyond my skill set. Which was bullshit. I was just as good a gamer as he ever was and had a larger audience when we'd met. But he had the almighty penis, and I was a woman in the gaming-sphere and had a much steeper battle than he ever had to deal with.

"I've never seen anything like this," Nathaniel said, wonder in his voice as he looked over my desk and recording supplies.

I bit back the inner bitch and thought about my setup from his point of view. He'd been in the Square since before YouTube gaming service even existed. Sure, game streaming had been a thing before he'd been cursed, but it was nothing like what we had now.

"That's my game streaming set up." I said, crossing the room to explain all of the systems and tools to him. His eyes went wide and practically glittered as he took in the set up.

"So, you're a game streamer?" He asked, fixed on the loading screen of one of my favorite adventure games. The graphics outstriped the Square graphics by miles.

"I was." I said, not wanting to talk about it.

"Why'd you stop?" He toggled the controller and entered the game. "This is so fucking cool."

He looked up at me then with a wide grin, not unlike a child on Christmas. "I bet you were awesome at it."

His eyes stayed locked on mine, and I relented. I sat on the floor and leaned back against the wall to watch him play.

"I was pretty damn good. My ex… well, he took all the fun out of it. And in the end, he put my name in the mud and I got too tired of dealing with the bullshit from the male viewers."

"So, some things never change." He set the controller down and turned in the chair to look down at me. "I'm sorry your ex was an ass. You don't deserve to lose something you love just because he has a tiny dick."

I laughed, but it felt a little hollow. "Play the game. Enjoy the technology advancements."

Nathaniel watched me for a long moment before the light in his eyes faded and he spun back to pick up the controller. I rested my head against the wall with a sigh and hated myself for getting involved with another gamer. There was no way I could go down this path again.

twelve

. . .

"I CALLED MY MOM TODAY," Nathaniel's announcement stopped me in my tracks as I left the office one day about a week after he emerged from the video game.

"Oh?" I accepted the energy drink he handed me and tried not to let my stomach fall to my ankles. "How did that go?"

"Weird." He rubbed a hand over his hair and sighed. "She seemed happy to hear from me but didn't seem to register that she hasn't seen me in a decade. It was like she knew the time had passed but she didn't really worry about my absence."

I thought about that. Would I want my family to miss me if I disappeared one day? I mean, yeah, but I also wouldn't want them to be worried. It was a hard call. And he was right, it was weird.

"Are you going to see her?" I asked. Nathaniel's family was only about two hours away.

"Eventually." He shrugged before wrapping his arms around his center. "Should I go now?"

There it was. The question we'd been dancing around for the last week. What happened now?

Nathaniel was a great houseguest. He cleaned

up after himself, helped in the kitchen on the days I was too tired to cook for myself, and didn't ask for much. Plus, the sex was still as phenomenal as it had been the first time.

We'd both tacitly avoided the question of what happened next since the moment he'd left me in the shower. It wasn't something I knew the answer to, or something I could expect of him.

Not after everything he'd been through.

"I mean, I'm sure your family would love to see you." I moved into the living room and sat in the arm chair. I curled my legs under me and gripped the can for dear life.

Nathaniel sat on the small couch and watched me carefully. "That's not what I asked."

I knew it wasn't. I knew what he was asking. I just didn't have an answer.

Was I willing to trust someone who had a clear passion for gaming and loved streaming as much as I did ever again? I'd just begun finding the joy in playing again since I'd bought the Square, and I didn't want to lose that. I didn't want to be in another highly competitive relationship again.

If Nathaniel had zero interest in video games, my answer would have been so simple. Yes. Yes, I wanted him to stay. Yes, I wanted to claim him as mine. Yes. Yes. Yes.

But it wasn't that simple. And while he hadn't brought up streaming to me directly, I'd found him more than once watching streamers and looking up how to do it from my old laptop. He had the game bug.

Didn't he deserve to do what he wanted with his life? Just because I didn't think I could handle dating in that situation again didn't mean I didn't want him to give it a go. He deserved to try things.

His entire life had been locked away from him for so long, who was I to keep him from exploring his options?

"I don't know." I finally said, voice quiet. "What do you want?"

"Easy." Nathaniel's eyes locked on mine, and the pale green was bright with some emotion that made me want to hide in my hoodie. "I want you."

"What if I'm not an option?" I asked, serious.

"Then I go see my family. Start over, I guess. Figure out what I can save from the life I had before." He shrugged like it was nothing, but I could tell it wasn't.

"But I think you should be an option. I think you're my best option. I think that you were meant to buy me and I think no one else would have been able to free me. I think you're the reason I'm back and the reason I get to stay." He fell to his knees and crawled to the chair. His hands were warm on my thighs as he gripped me. "For years, I waited in the dark and you brought me light. And yes, I am fucking grateful for that but that has so little to do with this."

My heart was in my throat as I carefully set my drink down on the carpet beside my chair. I didn't want to hear it. I never wanted him to stop.

"You're everything I've ever dreamed of in a girl. You're the player two I never imagined to find. So much so, that I never even bothered to look. I was young, dumb, and kind of a loser before I was cursed and now that I'm out I want to be better. I want to be someone worthwhile. I want to matter. And I want to matter to you."

His hands left my thighs to grip my fists. He waited until I loosened them enough so he could twine our fingers together.

"If it's the video games, I'll never play a single one again for as long as I live. As long as it means I get to have you." His voice was so sincere, his eyes bright. I wanted to believe him.

"You love them." I croaked out through the knot in my throat.

"I love you more."

My eyes went wide, and I nearly pulled away, but Nathaniel wouldn't let me.

He kept my hands tight in his grasp. "I love you, and I want forever with you. But if you're not ready for that, I'll go."

My heart raced in my ears as we sat there, holding hands. I watched the light go out of his eyes as the silence stretched on. And in that moment, I threw all my fears to the wind and said fuck it.

"Stay." I whispered. "Stay with me."

thirteen

· · ·

THE BELL over the door rang as Nathaniel and I walked into Retro Whimsy three weeks after he'd been freed from the video game.

Addy was behind the counter, and she looked up with a smile when we walked in. "Oh! You're back! I have something for you!"

I smiled at the exclamation points at the end of every sentence. It should have been annoying, but there was something so genuine about the woman I couldn't help but like her.

"Great." I smiled at her and squeezed Nathaniel's hand. "We're looking for some more video game systems."

She gave a little secret smile and nodded. "I take it the last one worked out for you?"

"Better than you could imagine." I told her, shooting the man next to me a wide smile.

"Well, go take a look! I'll get my thing from the back for you and meet you back there!" She disappeared behind some long black curtains, and I tugged Nathaniel down the aisle of the store to the back where the video game systems lived.

"Are you sure you're okay with this?" He asked,

checking in again. "We don't have to do this if you're not ready."

About a week ago he'd come up with an idea that was actually kind of genius. While I would never go back to my old gamer tag or stream the type of things I had before, I missed the community I'd created, and Nathaniel's idea was perfect for making a new one.

While there were many, many game streamers out there. There weren't many with a focus on playing the old games. The ones I'd grown up on. Nathaniel had been a champion at them before he'd been cursed.

Which is what brought us into Retro Whimsy. They had so many old systems just begging to be played, and we would do it. And stream our adventures.

"I'm so ready." And I was. Playing with Nathaniel was fun. He didn't make everything into a competition and was just as likely to cheer me on for being better than him as he was to celebrate his own wins.

Turns out, it wasn't that I was a poor player or sport. It was just that Sean was a complete and total asshole. I hoped him and his half-naked streaming fiance lived miserably ever after with each other. But he didn't have power over me and my decisions anymore.

"Here you go!" Addy was back, and she handed me a medium sized wooden box. It was intricately carved and had a seam along the top.

I opened it and handed the lid to Nathaniel before I began sorting through the contents. My eyes went wide and I looked to him.

"It's you." I said, holding the box out to him. He

traded me the lid for box and looked inside. His eyes flew to Addy.

"How?" He pulled out his driver's license and passport. "How did you get this?"

"We have our ways. Now, what games are we looking at today?" She rubbed her hands together and looked at the display of consoles like she hadn't just done something remarkable.

"That's not an answer." Nathaniel's voice was low and harsh. I put a hand on his arm to calm him. I didn't particularly care how or why she had it. I was just glad we had it now.

"The answer is not for you." Addy's voice lost all of its cheer, and the temperature in the store seemed to drop ten degrees. "Just say thank you and consider yourself lucky. Her latest boyfriend just spent two years as a glory hole. You got off easy."

Nathaniel's eyes went wide, and he took the lid from my hands and closed the box. "Thank you."

"That's better. Now, video games!" The cheer was back, and the lights seemed to get brighter as we looked over the systems available and picked three out.

Nathaniel was tense as we checked out, but he didn't say anything until we left the store with a smiling Addy waving us off.

"Do you think she's serious?" He asked, taking one of the bags from me and leading the way to the car.

"About the glory hole?"

"Yeah," he shuddered, and I didn't blame him. That seemed like a fate worse than death.

"How do you think that worked?" I asked, unlocking the doors and opening the truck for Nathaniel to store our systems and the box.

"I don't even want to know." He closed the trunk and turned to me. "And, as much as I feel bad for the guy, I can't help but want to thank Bethany for what she did to me."

I raised my eyebrows, not believing him for a moment. He smiled and wrapped his arms around my waist, pulling me into his body.

"If not for her, I wouldn't have you." He pressed a gentle kiss to my forehead, and I closed my eyes against the sweetness. "And I wouldn't trade a moment of time in that game away if it meant I didn't get to end up here."

"You're going to make me cry." I warned him, gripping his shirt and tilting my head up for a kiss.

"Let's go home."

epilogue

. . .

"DID you have to tell him about the glory hole?" Chloe asked as she came out of the back room. "What was the point?"

"He wasn't appreciative enough." Addy shrugged and began to hang the pile of clothes waiting for the racks. "We just gave the boy his freedom and he was questioning me."

"Addy," Chloe's voice held warning but, in the way of little sisters everywhere, Addy ignored it.

Chloe looked like she was gearing up for a lecture, so Addy was relieved when Lacey came down from the upstairs apartment the sisters shared. Their third sister looked concerned. Not a common look on their unflappable sister's face.

"What's happened?" Chloe asked, clearly seeing the same thing Addy saw.

"Nothing yet, but something is changing." Lacey tapped her fingers on the glass countertop and looked over the store of items they've been curating for centuries.

Chloe looked concerned, but Addy wasn't. Their plan would work. It had to. The universe was wildly unbalanced at the moment, and they needed this to work, to set the scales to rights.

And if she had a feeling in the pit of her stomach that something was about to happen? Well, she kept that to herself. Nothing good would come from worrying her sisters, and they couldn't do what needed to be done if they spent all their time waiting for something to happen.

"The next one is coming." Lacey said. "Soon."

Addy nodded in agreement. She wasn't sure which one it would be, but she knew someone's fate was about to change. She just wondered how many it would take before they could be done.

about the author

Sabrina Cross (she/her) is a neurospicy 80's baby from the middle of nowhere Michigan, where she still lives with her cat. She came into her monster romance era early when she fell in love with Beast from the 1997's X-Men animated series. After discovering sentient object romance in early 2023, Sabrina decided to embrace what she calls her 'Hold My Beer' style of writing and gave into the lifelong dream of being an author. When not writing weird monster/sentient object smut, Sabrina can be found hanging out on social media (@authorsabrinacross), reading, or hoarding office supplies.

also by sabrina cross

Yarn & Monsters Series

A True Love Spell Gone Wrong...

When four friends perform a true love spell, things go terribly wrong. Now they're locked into a deal with the devil and have only a year to find love and happiness or their souls are destined to face the flames. Armed with a demon guardian; Clover, Jasmine, Fern, and Violet are determined to beat the devil and save themselves. Except, this curse might be the best thing that's ever happened to them.

Corny: A F/F Candy Corn Romance

Snuggle: A M/F Demon Teddy Bear Romance

Tangled: A M/F Friends-To-Lovers Sentient Object Romance

Knotted: A M/F Demon Werewolf Romance

The Cursed Matchmaker Series

Never Piss off a witch. Or else you may find yourself trapped in a glory hole booth at an upscale sex club. But when the perfect couples hook up anonymously, Josh has no choice but to speak out and help them find love.

The Glory Whole Package

The Glory Whole Experiment

The Glory Whole Redemption

Retro Whimsy Series

Welcome to Retro Whimsy where nothing is as it seems and the owners know just what you need.

Getting Railed

Trogg Trouble

Ghostlight Falls - Shared World Series

Cooking Up A Demon

Stand Alone Monster Romance

Christmas with the Monster

Can't Yeti Enough

Stand Alone Sentient Object Romance

Light Me Up

Pounded by the Pommel Horse

Sentient Pen15 from Outer Space

Knotty Broomsticks

www.ingramcontent.com/pod-product-compliance
Lightning Source LLC
Chambersburg PA
CBHW020122310726
48970CB00002B/743